WOLF CHRISTMAS

by Daniel Pinkwater • illustrated by Jill Pinkwater

MARSHALL CAVENDISH • NEW YORK

I was sleeping with my brothers Tanglefoot and Peewee. We were warm and cozy, snuggling under the snow. Momma was sleeping nearby, and Aunt Fang, and our older brother, Robert, all covered by mounds of snow.

Poppa was somewhere nearby, watching over us. There was a bright moon. We had all had a good meal of venison Poppa had caught earlier. Peewee and Tanglefoot made contented little growls and mumbling noises in their sleep.

Peewee stretched. I felt his four paws push against me, shoving me out of the warm tangle of fur. I growled a cranky growl. Tanglefoot heard me growl, and bit Peewee on the tail.

Then, all at once, we exploded out of our snow mound. We were wide awake, wrestling and tumbling, jumping on one another, laughing and biting and pushing.

Peewee found a twig, and Tanglefoot and I chased him. First   Tanglefoot had
the twig and then I had it. We scampered about, bumping into the grown-up wolves,
growling and yelping.

Momma and Aunt Fang and Robert stood up and shook the snow off their backs, and
then settled down again, watching us play in the moonlight.

Sometimes we were able to get the grown-up wolves to join us and play too. Tonight when I would bump into one of them and fall on my side and then roll on my back with my paws waving in the air, the big wolf would nuzzle me, but not get up and romp.

Poppa appeared out of a little stand of trees. We stopped our game and ran up to him. We reached up and rubbed our faces against his face.

"Uncle Louis is coming," Poppa said.

"Whee! Uncle Louis!" we pups said. We loved Uncle Louis. He was a funny wolf, and always had interesting things to tell us and show us.

"How do you know Uncle Louis is coming?" Robert asked. "Did you see him? Did you smell him? Did you hear him howl?"

"I just know," Poppa said.

"It will be nice to see Uncle Louis," Momma said.

"Yes," Poppa said. "Though he is not a serious wolf."

"The pups like him," Momma said.

"We love Uncle Louis!" we pups said.

A little while later Uncle Louis appeared. We pups did not approach him with respect the way we approached Poppa. We flew at him, jumped all over him, and rolled him in the snow. Uncle Louis laughed and batted us with his paws.

"What big pups!" Uncle Louis said. "And what a pretty wolf little Stinkface has become." Stinkface is my name. I felt my fur tingle when Uncle Louis said I was pretty.

Uncle Louis rubbed faces with the big wolves, just a little rub with Poppa and Momma—Robert and Aunt Fang approached with their legs bent and heads held sideways, and reached up to rub faces almost like pups. Uncle Louis is black all over, with yellow eyes, and he is very tall.

"It's the longest night of the year, or just about," Uncle Louis said. "Does everyone feel like taking a run through the woods? I want to show you something unusual."

"Louis, you have not been going near that pack of humans again, have you? They are dangerous to wolves."

"They are hardly dangerous," Uncle Louis said. "They are so clumsy and make so much noise, they are not able to get near us or even see us if we don't want them to. Besides, this is their special night. They are quite peaceful and won't be bothering about wolves."

"Oh please, Poppa! Let us run through the woods with Uncle Louis and see something unusual!" we all yelped.

"It is a fine night," Poppa said. "I must admit I do feel like running."

And we were off, all of us, bounding through the woods.

The snow felt crisp and crunchy under our feet. The moon made dark shadows. We breathed the cold air deep into our lungs. I stretched my long legs out. I felt strong. I felt light. The moon shone silver on my brothers' fur, and the stars were bright. We never got tired. I felt as though we could run forever.

We smelled the place where the humans lived. There were about a hundred smells we had never smelled before, and some of them were nice. Then we stopped and sat on a hillside. Below us was the humans' place.

The humans live in big wooden things. Uncle Louis said they put pieces of wood together to make them. They have light in them, and it shines out through holes in the sides. And there were colored lights, like colored stars, everywhere. And hot smoky smells, and strange meat smells, and sweet smells.

We didn't see any humans. They were inside the wooden things with the light shining out through the holes and the glittering lights on the outsides and the smoke coming out and the snow on top.

We didn't see the humans, but we could hear them. They were singing. We listened. It was nice. I thought, Even if they are dangerous, they are animals, just like we are.

Then we threw back our heads and, sitting on the hillside above the place where the humans live, we wolves sang too.

For Arctic Flake

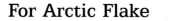

Marshall Cavendish, 99 White Plains Road, Tarrytown, New York 10591
The text of this book is set in 16 point Egyptian 505 Medium.
The illustrations are rendered in felt markers.
Printed in Hong Kong
6 5 4 3

Library of Congress Cataloging-in-Publication Data
Pinkwater, Daniel Manus, date.
Wolf Christmas / by Daniel Pinkwater ; illustrations by Jill Pinkwater.   p. cm.
Summary: On the longest night of the year, a family of wolves takes a run through
the woods to see the unusual sight of a human family's Christmas celebration.
ISBN 0-7614-5030-0   [1. Wolves—Fiction. 2. Christmas—Fiction.]
I. Pinkwater, Jill, ill. II. Title.
PZ7.P6335W1   1998   [E]—dc21   97-50363   CIP   AC